P9-CNC-202

WEEKLY READER
CHILDREN'S BOOK CLUB

WEEKLY READER CHILDREN'S BOOK CLUB presents

HARRY
by the Sea

HARRY

by Gene Zion

HARPER & ROW, PUBLISHERS

by the Sea

Pictures by **Margaret Bloy Graham**

NEW YORK, EVANSTON, AND LONDON

HARRY BY THE SEA
Text copyright © 1965 by Eugene Zion
Pictures copyright © 1965 by Margaret Bloy Graham
Printed in the United States of America for
Harper & Row, Publishers, Incorporated.
All rights reserved.
Library of Congress Catalog Card Number: 65-21302

Weekly Reader Children's Book Club Edition
Primary Division

Harry was a white dog with black spots
who liked everything about the seashore,
except...the hot sun.
One day when the sun was hotter than ever,
Harry looked for a shady place to sit.
But when he tried to get under
the family's beach umbrella...

it was too crowded and the family made him leave.

When he crawled into the children's sand castle...

the walls fell in and the children chased him away.

When he walked in the shade that a fat lady made...

she became angry and made him stop following her.

"Get lost!" she said. She was very annoyed.

The sun was very hot and Harry had walked
a long way from the main beach.
He was tired, so he sat down at the water's edge.

All of a sudden a big wave came from behind
and crashed right on top of him.

When the wave rolled back, Harry was left floating
in the water. He was completely covered with seaweed.
He didn't look like a dog anymore—
he looked like something from the bottom of the sea.

When he got there, Harry stopped and stared. Instead of
just his family's umbrella, now there were hundreds
of them. They were <u>all</u> striped—just like his family's.
Harry couldn't tell one umbrella from another.

On his way, some people saw him.
"It's a Sea Serpent!" one of them screamed.
"It's a Giant Sandworm!" shrieked another.
Harry had water in his ears and could hardly hear them.
He kept on running toward the main beach.

Everyone ran out of the water, and so did Harry.
He was still covered with cold, wet seaweed.
It made him feel cool and comfortable, and now
he didn't mind the sun at all. He felt so good,
he started running back to his family.

Suddenly a lady saw him floating toward her.
"Help! Help!" she shrieked. "It's a Sea Monster!"
The lifeguard heard her and blew his whistle.
"Everybody out!" he shouted. "Everybody out!"

Suddenly two beach attendants saw him.
"Holy smoke!" one of them gasped. "What's that?"
"It's a Bushy-backed Sea Slug!" exclaimed the other.
They whispered for a moment. Then they ran.

Harry went from umbrella to umbrella, but he couldn't find his family. <u>Everyone</u> wore sun hats and sunglasses, and <u>everyone</u> used suntan oil—just like his family. Harry looked and sniffed very hard, but it was no use. He couldn't tell one family from another.

Suddenly the two beach attendants came running back carrying a big trash basket. They ran toward Harry. "Stand back!" one of them said to the crowd. "We're going to catch it and take it to the Aquarium!" said the other.

Then they tiptoed right up behind Harry
and raised the trash basket over his head.
Harry didn't know the beach attendants were
behind him. He was listening to something.

He thought he heard someone calling his name.
There it was again. "Harry! Harry! Harry!"
Now Harry was sure. He didn't wait another second.
Just as the basket came down —

he ran! He ran right out from under the basket!
It happened so fast, the beach attendants
just stood there with their mouths open.

As he raced through the crowd some people screamed,
some people ran, and some people did both. But Harry
paid no attention. He kept on running across the beach.

When he got to the Hot Dog stand,
he stopped and barked happily.
Behind the counter the Hot Dog man was shouting.
It was <u>his</u> voice that Harry had heard. But Harry had
water in his ears and couldn't hear very well.

The man wasn't shouting, "Harry! Harry! Harry!"
He was shouting, "Hurry! Hurry! Hurry! Get 'em while
they're hot!" Harry still thought the man was
calling his name. He barked and jumped with joy.
He jumped so much that suddenly...

the seaweed all fell off!
When the crowd saw that Harry was a dog,
they gasped. They could hardly believe their eyes.
All at once Harry began to jump higher than ever.

He saw the children! They were running toward him.
"Oh, Harry!" they cried. "We heard you bark!"
"We've been looking all over for you!"
Harry was so happy, he did a little dance.

The Hot Dog man was very grateful to Harry
for bringing the crowd to his stand. He sold all
the hot dogs he had. He gave Harry a free hamburger.
The lady who had told Harry to "get lost" came along
and bought him a cold drink.

"You're no Sea Monster," she said. "You're just a lost, hot dog." Everyone laughed except the two children.
"He's <u>not</u> lost!" one of them said.
"He's <u>Harry</u> and he's <u>ours</u>!"
Then they hurried off to join the rest of the family.

The next time Harry's family went to the beach,
they brought a new umbrella. Harry liked this one
very much. It was white with black spots.
No matter how crowded the beach became,
it was easy to find. But best of all—it was big,
and when the sun got very hot,
there was room underneath for them all.